THE POPPY SEEDS

As Pablo went close to the spri

Pablo jumped. The poppy see

He looked around. Old Antonio had come out of the house. His eyes were red and angry. He had a stick in his hand and he beat on the ground with it.

"Who are you, and what are you doing here?" he asked.

"My—my name is Pablo, sir," said Pablo. "I came to plant some poppy seeds in your yard."

"Poppy seeds?" said the old man.

"Yes," said Pablo, "but I dropped them. Now they are lost in the grass."

"Poppy seeds—ha! Did you think I would believe such a story as that?" said the old man. "I know why you came here. You were going to steal water from the spring."

"Oh, no!" said Pablo.

"Oh, yes!" cried Old Antonio. "Get out, and if I ever find you here again, I'll—"

Pablo did not wait to hear the rest. He ran out through the gate and down the road.

The Poppy Seeds

The Poppy Seeds

by CLYDE ROBERT BULLA

illustrated by JEAN CHARLOT

PUFFIN BOOKS

PUFFIN BOOKS

Published by the Penguin Group

Penguin Books USA Inc., 375 Hudson Street, New York, New York 10014, U.S.A.

Penguin Books Ltd, 27 Wrights Lane, London W8 5TZ, England

Penguin Books Australia Ltd, Ringwood, Victoria, Australia

Penguin Books Canada Ltd, 10 Alcorn Avenue, Toronto, Ontario, Canada M4V 3B2

Penguin Books (N.Z.) Ltd, 182-190 Wairau Road, Auckland 10, New Zealand

Penguin Books Ltd, Registered Offices: Harmondsworth, Middlesex, England

First published in the United States of America by Thomas Y. Crowell Company, 1955
Published in Puffin Books, 1994

7 9 10 8 6

LIBRARY OF CONGRESS CATALOGING-IN-PUBLICATION DATA

Bulla, Clyde Robert.

The poppy seeds / by Clyde Robert Bulla; illustrated by Jean Charlot.

p.   cm.

Summary: A young boy's attempts to grow poppies in his drought parched village
soften the heart of the grouchy old man who has the village's only spring in his back yard.

ISBN 0-14-036731-4

[1. Mexico—Fiction.] I. Charlot, Jean, ill. II. Title.

PZ7.B912Po   1994   [Fic]—dc20   94-16921   CIP   AC

Printed in the United States of America

For Peter Charlot
born in Mexico

The Poppy Seeds

IN a valley at the foot of a mountain lived a boy named Pablo. His home was a little brick house with a roof of banana leaves. There were holes in the sides of the house and holes in the roof, but no one cared. The valley was never cold, and it never rained there.

Pablo used to say to himself, "If only it would rain!"

Then the valley would not be dusty and brown. Grass would grow and flowers would bloom. It would be the most beautiful valley in all Mexico. And he could catch the rain in pans and jars. Then he would not have to go to the river for water.

Every day he took two big jars to the river. He filled them with water and brought them home. He carried them on a yoke that went over his shoulder. It was a heavy load, and the river was a long way off. The yoke always hurt his shoulder, and he had to rest a long time after he got home.

Sometimes Mother would say, "Stay here today. I'll go to the river." Or Father would say, "I'll get the water today."

But Pablo knew how hard Mother worked, doing the cooking and keeping the house. He knew how hard Father worked in the fields on the other side of the mountain. So he always said, "No. Getting the water is my work."

All the people in the valley used water from the river. All the people except one man. That man was Old Antonio.

Old Antonio lived alone in a house beside the mountain. He had no need of the warm, muddy water in the river. He had a spring in his own back yard.

It was a spring of clear, cold water. It came from the foot of the mountain, ran a little way, and disappeared among the rocks.

When people went past Old Antonio's house, they heard the spring running over the rocks. They liked to hear the sound it made, but they never stopped for a drink of the cold, fresh water. Old Antonio had built a high wall around his land. If people came to his gate, he drove them away.

"You only stop because you want to drink from my spring," he said. "If everyone came here to drink, there would not be enough water left for me. Go away, and leave me alone."

So the people of the valley left him alone.

One morning Pablo took the two big jars to the river. He dipped them into the water and filled them. He sat down on a rock to rest before he started back.

While he sat there, he thought he heard someone crying.

He listened. The sound came from around the bend of the river.

He looked around the bend. There by the river sat a girl. She was crying, with her hands over her face.

"Girl!" said Pablo.

She looked up at him.

"Are you hurt?" he asked.

She shook her head.

"Are you lost?"

"No."

"Then why are you crying?"

"I lost my cup!" said the girl, and she began to cry harder than ever.

"Was it only a cup you lost?" said Pablo. "I can get you another one from home."

"Oh, but not like this one," said the girl. "There is not another cup like it in all the world. My grandmother made it for me when I was a baby. She put my name on it."

"How did you lose it?" asked Pablo.

"When I dipped up some water," said the girl, "the cup fell out of my hand."

"Where were you when it fell out of your hand?" asked Pablo.

"Here by this big rock," said the girl.

Pablo lay down on the rock. He put his hand and arm into the river. Down he reached, farther and farther, until his head was under the water. He touched the bottom of the river. He touched something round and smooth.

He brought it up out of the water. It was only a stone.

Again he reached down into the water. This time he touched something round and smooth that had a handle. He brought it out of the water.

It was a little brown cup with blue flowers on it. The name on it was "Lolita."

"My cup!" cried the girl. "Oh, my pretty little cup! I thought I would never see you again!"

She held the cup close to her and went running away. Then she came back. "Thank you," she said. "Here— this is for you."

She put a handkerchief into Pablo's hand. "Good-by," she said, and ran away again.

Pablo looked at the handkerchief. There was something tied up in one corner of it.

He untied the knot. In the corner of the handkerchief were dozens of little black seeds.

When he got home with the water, he showed the seeds to Mother.

"What kind are they?" he asked.

"They are poppy seeds," she told him.

"Will flowers grow from them?" asked Pablo.

"They will not grow here," said Mother. "The ground is too hard and dry, and we have not enough water to make them grow."

"I'm going to plant them," said Pablo. "Maybe it will rain this year. Then the poppies will grow."

He took a stick and scratched a place in the ground. As he started to plant the seeds, he looked up the road at the other houses. He thought how beautiful the valley would look with poppies growing by every house.

"Mother!" he called, "I'm going to plant some seeds by every house!"

Mother smiled. It was a sad smile. "Run along, my son," she said. "Make all the valley beautiful."

Pablo went up the road. At every house he stopped and planted a few poppy seeds.

People smiled and shook their heads. "Poppies won't grow here, Pablo. The valley is too dry."

"But maybe this year it will rain," said Pablo.

There were only five seeds left when he came to the last house on the road. It was old Antonio's house.

Pablo looked at the high wall that kept everyone out. He felt a little sorry for the old man who lived there alone.

He said to himself, "I'm not afraid of him. I'll plant some poppies in his yard, too."

The big gate was closed. He gave it a push. It was not locked.

He gave it another push. It opened wide enough that he could slip through.

He saw no one in Old Antonio's yard. He heard nothing except the sound of water running over stones.

He went around the house and into the back yard.
And there he saw the spring!

Out of the foot of the mountain came the stream
of water. It was not like any water Pablo had ever seen
before. It was clear and bright. Where the sun shone
on it, it looked like silver.

Grass grew beside the stream. Near the place where
the water disappeared, a banana tree spread its cool
green leaves.

As Pablo went close to the spring, someone shouted,
"Stop!"

Pablo jumped. The poppy seeds fell out of his hand.

He looked around. Old Antonio had come out of the house. His eyes were red and angry. He had a stick in his hand and he beat on the ground with it.

"Who are you, and what are you doing here?" he asked.

"My—my name is Pablo, sir," said Pablo. "I came to plant some poppy seeds in your yard."

"Poppy seeds?" said the old man.

"Yes," said Pablo, "but I dropped them. Now they are lost in the grass."

"Poppy seeds — *ha!* Did you think I would believe such a story as that?" said the old man. "I know why you came here. You were going to steal water from my spring!"

"Oh, no!" said Pablo.

"Oh, yes!" cried Old Antonio. "Get out, and if I ever find you here again, I'll—"

Pablo did not wait to hear the rest. He ran out through the gate and down the road.

When he got home, Mother asked him, "Did you plant all your poppy seeds?"

"All but five," said Pablo. "I lost them."

"You look tired," said Mother. "I think you have been too long in the hot sun. Come in and lie down."

Pablo lay down. He went to sleep. He dreamed he was in Old Antonio's yard and the old man was shouting, "Poppy seeds—ha! You came here to steal water from my spring!"

"No!" said Pablo. "No, no!"

Mother came to the bed and looked down at him. She did not know why he was saying, "No, no, no!" in his sleep.

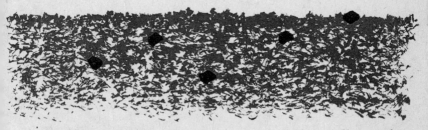

Weeks went by. No rain came to the valley. The poppy seeds Pablo had planted dried up in the ground.

One morning Old Antonio went to his spring to get a jar of water. In the grass at his feet he saw something red. He bent over it. It was a poppy.

Close beside it were two more poppies. Three red poppies in his back yard!

As he looked at them, he thought of times long ago when he was a boy. He had lived in a big house with his mother and father and many brothers and sisters. They had all been happy together. And always, in front of the house, there had been beds of poppies—bright red poppies like these.

But how had they got here?

Then he remembered. A boy named Pablo had come into his yard. "I came to plant some poppy seeds," he had said.

"You were going to steal water from my spring!" Old Antonio had said. He had driven the boy away.

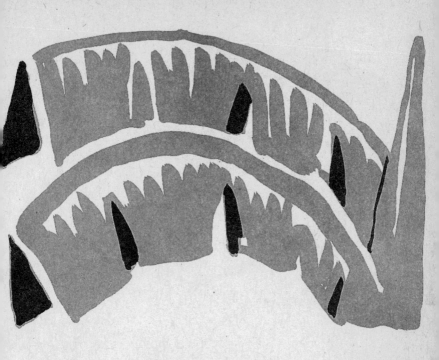

He sat down under the banana tree. For a long time he looked at the red poppies.

Now he wished he had not driven the boy away. "If he comes back," he thought, "I will let him drink from my spring."

Every day the old man watched by his gate. He saw people go up and down the road, but he did not see the boy.

One day he saw a man riding a donkey down the road. He called to him, "Do you know a boy named Pablo?"

"I know him well," said the man. "He lives in the house at the far end of the valley."

"When you see him, will you tell him this?" said Old Antonio. "Tell him to stop here the next time he comes this way."

"That may be a long time," said the man. "Pablo is sick. He has been in his bed ever since the day he planted poppy seeds by every house in the valley. Some say he stayed too long in the hot sun."

The man rode away.

Old Antonio went to the spring. He dipped up a jar of water. He wrapped it in leaves to keep it cool. There were more poppies now and he picked a little bunch. With the jar under his arm and the poppies in his hand, he started down the road.

He could not walk fast. It was an hour before he came to Pablo's house.

When Mother saw Old Antonio, she was so sur-
prised she did not know what to say.

"I have come to see the boy Pablo," said the old man.

"Yes, sir," said Mother.

She stood aside for Old Antonio to come in.

Pablo lay in his bed. His eyes were closed. The old man put the poppies down on the pillow.

Pablo opened his eyes. "Poppies!" he cried. "Are they from the seeds I planted? Have my poppies bloomed?"

"Yes," said the old man. "And look. Here is water from my spring."

Pablo looked up at Old Antonio. At first he was afraid.

"Can you say 'thank you,' Pablo?" said, Mother.

"Thank you," said Pablo. He was not afraid any longer because he saw that the old man was trying to be kind.

He drank a cup of the fresh spring water.

"It is good," he said. "I never knew water could be so good."

From that day Pablo grew stronger.

When he was well again, he went to see Old Antonio.

"Take your water from the spring," the old man told him. "Then you won't have to go all the way to the river."

So Pablo filled his jars from the spring.

"Ask your father to help me dig a little ditch," said Old Antonio. "Then you won't have to carry the jars all the way up the road and back."

Pablo's father and the old man began to dig a ditch along the side of the road. Some of the neighbors helped.

Before long there was water running all the way from the spring to Pablo's house.

"See how much water there is!" said Pablo. "There is enough for all."

"Do you think so?" asked the old man. "Let us see." He told the neighbors, "Take some of the water for yourselves."

The neighbors began to take water from the little ditch. There was enough for them to drink. There was even enough for them to water a small garden in each yard.

"There *is* enough for all," said the old man.

"This good water is a present from Old Antonio," said the people.

Everyone in the valley was the old man's friend. And his best friend of all was the boy Pablo.

OTHER PUFFIN BOOKS YOU MAY ENJOY: